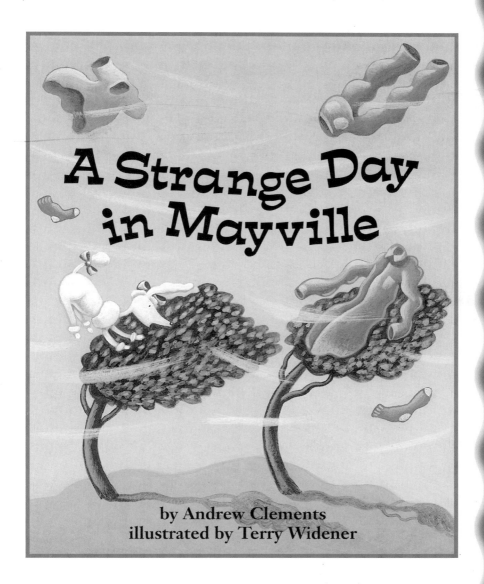

A Strange Day in Mayville

by Andrew Clements
illustrated by Terry Widener

 HOUGHTON MIFFLIN   BOSTON

It was a summer day in Mayville. The sun
was bright. It was warm. All the people in town
were busy doing the things they always do.

Then a big gust of wind came to town.
People in Mayville know just where they were
when the gust came.

3

Jean Adams had a white dog. The dog's name was Clipper. It was a good name, because Jean liked to clip the dog's hair.

Jean was clipping her dog when the big gust came. Clipper yawned and the big gust blew into her mouth.

Clipper grew bigger and bigger. She looked like a big white balloon. Then the big gust blew Clipper away. Jean tried to catch her.

A man called the police. "Help!" he yelled. "A big white balloon is chasing me. It barks like a dog!"

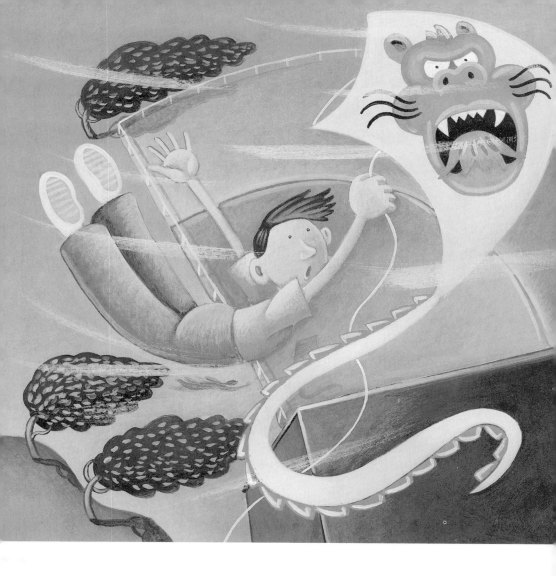

Tommy James was flying his kite in the park
when the big gust came. The wind picked up the kite.
Tommy was holding the kite, so he went up too!

Tommy and his kite flew over the school. Tommy saw a flagpole. He grabbed the pole with his legs and let go of the kite. He slid down the pole.

Elsie Chen was in her garden when the big gust came. Her hat flew off her head. She turned her head to look for it.

Then she turned back to her garden. The garden was gone! "My garden! Where did it go?" she yelled.

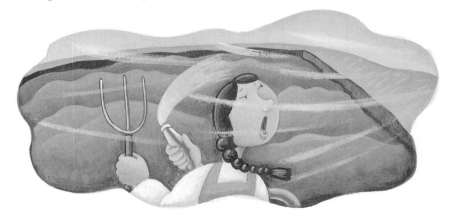

Elsie looked around and saw her garden on the roof of her house. Elsie was happy. "That is not so bad," she said. "Now my plants will have more sun."

Elsie gave her garden a lot of water. Her tomatoes grew very big. Elsie won first prize at the county fair!

Some kids were playing in the school gym when the big gust came. The doors opened, and you'll never believe what happened. A whole pond blew in, with six lily pads, three ducks, three frogs, and one tall man in a little red boat!

The kids and the tall man played in the water. The ducks and frogs sat in the boat and watched the kids playing. The lily pads just sat there, as they always do.

Bob Belcher was mowing his lawn when the big gust came. It blew Bob and his lawnmower all over town. Bob and his mower cut all the grass in Mayville.

The big gust blew the grass around. The grass landed on the steps of the library and made a nice green pile. Soon all the children came to read on the soft, nice-smelling green pile.

Jane Asher was in the Sport Shop. She was putting away some tennis balls when the big gust came. It blew them out the door and into the sky, along with all the other balls from the store.

Tim Lewis reported the news. He was outside giving the weather report. "It is a strange day in Mayville," he said. "There is a big gust. There are balls falling from the sky! Tennis balls! Softballs! Footballs! Basketballs! BOWLING BALLS! HELP!"

Gary Jones was fixing his fence when the big gust came. All of the wood and the box of nails flew into the sky. When they all came down, Gary had a new fence! It looked very neat.

Gary liked his new fence. After that day, he tried to make more fences the same way. He juggled the wood, hammer, and nails. He did not make any more fences, but he became a great juggler!

People in Mayville wondered what the gust would do next. But it just went away.

Strange things still happen in Mayville. But nothing has been as strange as that big gust!